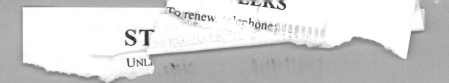

For Celia

Other books about Alfie:

Alfie Gets in First
Alfie's Feet
Alfie Gives a Hand
An Evening at Alfie's
Alfie and the Birthday Surprise
Alfie Weather
Annie Rose is my Little Sister
The Big Alfie and Annie Rose Storybook
The Big Alfie Out of Doors Storybook
Rhymes for Annie Rose
Alfie's Alphabet
Alfie's Numbers

Alfie Wins a Prize
A Bodley Head Book 0 370 32824 8
Published in Great Britain by The Bodley Head,
an imprint of Random House Children's Books
This edition published 2004.
1 3 5 7 9 10 8 6 4 2
Copyright © Shirley Hughes, 2004
The right of Shirley Hughes to be identified as the author and illustrator
of this work has been asserted in accordance with the Copyright,
Designs and Patents Act 1988. All rights reserved.
Random House Children's Books, 61–63 Uxbridge Road, London W5 5SA
A division of The Random House Group Ltd
Random House Australia (PTY) Ltd, 20 Alfred Street, Milsons Point,
Sydney, New South Wales 2061, Australia
Random House New Zealand Ltd, 18 Poland Road, Glenfield,
Auckland 10, New Zealand
Random House (PTY) Ltd, Endulini, 5A Jubilee Road, Parktown 2193,
South Africa
THE RANDOM HOUSE GROUP Limited Reg. No. 954009
www.kidsatrandomhouse.co.uk
A CIP catalogue record for this book is available from the British Library.
Printed in China

ALFIE
Wins a
Prize

Shirley Hughes

THE BODLEY HEAD

LONDON

One Saturday morning when Alfie and Annie Rose had finished their breakfast, Dad said he was thinking of taking them to the Harvest Fair at the Big School that afternoon. Alfie and Annie Rose liked fairs, where there were usually interesting things to look at and good things to eat.

"There's going to be a pet show and a children's painting competition too," Dad told Alfie.

Alfie wanted to take their cat Chessie along and put her into the pet show. He was sure she would win a prize. But Mum said that Chessie wasn't the sort of cat who would like being in a show, and that it might put her into a cross mood.

"What about painting a picture instead?" Dad suggested.

Alfie thought that was a good idea. He liked painting. Mum found a piece of paper and a paint brush and they cleared a space on the table. Then they got out the paints that Grandma had given them and Mum showed Alfie how to wash out his brush so the colours would not get mixed up and turn muddy.

"What shall I paint?" Alfie asked.
   Mum thought. Then she fetched the jug, which had yellow and orange leaves, red berries and mauve daisy flowers in it, and put it on the table. "These are pretty, don't you think?" she said.

But Alfie did not want to paint leaves and berries. He already
had a better idea. He dipped his brush carefully into the paint
and began his picture.

When he had finished, everyone was very interested to see what he had painted. "I like all that red and black," said Dad. "It's a face, I can see that. Is it some sort of bird?"

"No," said Alfie, "it's a motorbike man. These are his eyes and this is his red helmet. And these are his black gloves."

Mum helped Alfie to write his name under his picture. Then she wrote at the top: "Children's Painting Competition: 5 and Under, MOTORBIKE MAN". And she stuck the picture up on the door of the fridge so that they could all admire it while they had lunch. Then they set out for the Harvest Fair. Alfie carried his painting, carefully rolled.

The first people they saw in the Big School hall were Maureen NacNally and her mum. They had made an enormous cake and were inviting people to guess how much it weighed. The person who guessed nearest was going to win the cake.

Then Alfie and Mum and Dad and Annie Rose went to look at all the flowers and fruit and vegetables,

and second-hand toys,

and home-made cakes and fudge.

Then they went into the school playground
to look at the pet show.

Min and her little sister Lily had brought their beautiful
rabbits. They let Alfie and Annie Rose stroke them.
The white rabbit, Bianca, had pink eyes. Domino's eyes
were like shiny dark brown beads.

Bernard had put his pet beetle into the show. It lived in a jam jar amongst a lot of leaves.

"You can't see him because he's hiding," Bernard told Alfie. "He may come out later if he feels like it."

Bernard was going in for the children's painting competition too, so they all went off together. When they got there Bernard unrolled his picture and held it up for Alfie and Annie Rose to see. "It's two slime monsters having a fight," he told them.

Bernard was not a careful painter. There was a lot of slime and red blood dripping all over the picture. But Alfie and Annie Rose thought it was very good.

A lot of other children were handing in their pictures and a teacher was pinning them up on big screens.

Alfie's "Motorbike Man" was pinned up with the other pictures. Everyone was gathering round to look.

Some children had done cars, trucks and spaceships. The Santos twins had both painted bugs and butterflies.

Kevin Turley had done a picture of his mum. Louise Harper had painted a blue house with a lot of smoke coming out of the chimney, and Rahima Shariff had done a beautiful picture of orange and yellow leaves and berries and a big red apple.

On a table nearby were the prizes. The first prize for
the Five and Unders was a picture book about dinosaurs.
The second prize was a jigsaw puzzle of a farmyard scene
and the third prize was a bottle of bright green bubble
bath. Behind them sat a sad, stuffed, woolly animal.
Alfie was not sure whether he was a sheep or a goat.

"He's a consolation prize," Mum explained.
"That's a cheer-up prize for someone
who's not won but tried
very hard."

The consolation prize's ears were lopsided, and he wore a jersey with orange buttons. Alfie stared at him but he didn't look back. He had his nose in the air, as if he were trying not to mind about not being a proper prize like the others.

Everyone waited around while the judges looked at the pictures.

But now at last the winners were being announced!

First prize – Rahima Shariff!

Second prize – Kevin Turley!

Third prize –

Alfie!

Everyone clapped and cheered. Alfie stepped up all by himself
and shook hands with the lady who was presenting the prizes.
She gave him the green bubble bath and told him that she thought
his picture was "colourful and original". Last of all it was announced
that the consolation prize went to Louise for her blue house.
It was all very exciting. Alfie's friends
crowded around him. All except
Bernard, that is.

He was very upset that his
painting of slime monsters
had not won. He told Alfie
that he thought all the
prizes were silly.

Louise was not at all happy either.

"She's rather down in the dumps, I'm afraid," her dad told Alfie's dad later when they were having tea together. "She had set her heart on the green bubble bath."

"Soft toys are babyish," said Louise.

And she shoved the consolation prize down on the floor
beside her chair. He sat there with his nose still proudly
in the air. Of course, Alfie knew that toys cannot understand
anything. But secretly he hoped that the sheep (or goat)'s
feelings were not hurt because Louise did not want him.

Alfie felt a tiny bit sorry for
Louise too. She was so cross
and disappointed. Then he
quietly made up his mind.
He slipped off his chair and
went to whisper in Dad's ear.

"Alfie has a suggestion to
make," said Dad out loud.

Alfie went over to Louise
and said, "I'll swap my
bubble bath for your
prize if you like."

Louise thought that
was an excellent idea.
So they swapped
prizes right away.

Now Louise was all smiles.
She said she was going
to ask Alfie to tea at her
house next Saturday and
let him have a go on her
new trampoline.

Then they waved
goodbye, Louise
clutching her bubble
bath and Alfie holding
the consolation prize
tightly in his arms.

When the Harvest Fair was over the children who had
painted pictures were allowed to take them home.
Alfie carried his painting carefully rolled under one
arm and his consolation prize under the other.

On the way out they met Bernard, looking very pleased with himself.

"My beetle has won a prize for being the smallest pet," he told Alfie. "And I got a packet of chocolate buttons."

Alfie and Annie Rose looked into the jam jar. But they still could not see Bernard's prize-winning beetle, only leaves.

"He's had a very exciting day," said Bernard. "He may be feeling a bit tired."

Then he gave Alfie and Annie Rose two chocolate buttons each.

As soon as they got home Annie Rose wanted to do a painting of her own. Luckily there was plenty of paint left in the palette. When she had finished she made Mum stick her picture up on the fridge too, underneath Alfie's.

Alfie sat his prize on the window sill next to his old knitted elephant, Flumbo.

"What will you call him?" Dad wanted to know.

Alfie thought for a while. He was remembering a name he had often seen on a bus which passed near their street, which he had asked Mum to spell out for him. He liked the sound of it.

"His name is Willesden," he told them all.

"I think that suits him very well," said Mum.

And that is how Willesden stopped being a consolation prize and became part of the family.

The artwork for this book
was done in gouache colour
combined with oil pastels.